Dracula Investigates...

written and illustrated

by

Andy Bruce

ISBN: 1503053261
ISBN-13: 978-1503053267

For Wendy and Erin,

my beautiful wife and daughter.

Thank you for your love and support.

I know I can always *COUNT* on you!.

All characters and events in this work, alive or ***undead***,
are fictitious

---------- CONTENTS ----------

Dracula Investigates…
The Night of the Living Ted

Dracula Investigates...
The Night of the living Ted

CHAPTER 1

The moon shone in the night sky, its bright white beams cutting through the dark clouds onto the empty streets of Transylvania below. The only other light came from gas lamps dotted around the town; the darkened windows of houses and shops stared out at each other like the eye sockets of skulls.

The town slept... or at least *nearly* all the town slept. From one particular street, or rather from below one particular street at the corner of the town bank, the muffled sound of stone being chipped by metal could be heard. For down in a candle-lit cellar, two men were attacking a stone wall with pick axes trying to break their way through.

"How much longer, Daniel?" asked one of the men in a gruff voice. He lowered his pick axe and stretched. "I don't know how much more I can do."

He was a young man with tangled ginger hair that had matted to his forehead with sweat. His partner in crime was older with white hair and a thin moustache across his tough face.

"Another half an hour... if you keep up!" he hissed while still swinging his axe. "Once we're through... (*CLANK*) we'll be able to get... (*CLANK*) into the bank vault!"

The younger man raised his axe once again but before he took a swing at the wall, he stopped. He turned his head, listening.

"What's wrong now, Stefan?" asked Daniel, finally taking a break from his work.

"I thought I heard something."

They both stood still in the gloomy candlelight trying not to breathe too heavily while they listened. All seemed quiet.

"It was probably just a rat," said Daniel.

"I suppose so," replied Stefan, and they both resumed their work, chipping away at the wall. However they weren't alone. They were being watched by a small pair of red eyes that stared down at them from a high wooden beam - but this was no rat!

"Gentlemen..." a mysterious voice echoed round the cellar, "I don't believe you should be doing that."

The thieves quickly turned and raised their axes

as weapons, staring into the gloom to locate the source of the voice.

"Who's there!?" cried Daniel.

"It's him!" screamed Stefan, panic in his voice.

"Please put down your tools," came the reply in a very calm yet booming voice.

"What do we do?!" whimpered Stefan, the sweat dripping from his brow.

"He doesn't scare me!" shouted Daniel, swinging his pick axe in front of him.

"Do not make this harder for yourselves," came the voice, and a bat hopped off the beam and landed on the floor behind them. As the two men continued to stare into the dark corners of the cellar, the bat transformed into a tall thin man dressed in an evening suit with a long black cape. He had pale skin that appeared deathly white in the candle light.

Count Dracula was now towering over the criminals, his red eyes staring down at the back of their heads. Slowly he leaned in between the two frightened men and gently whispered *"BOO!"*

Screaming, they both dropped their pick axes with a loud *CLANG!* and ran to the cellar door.

"Let me out of here!!" cried Stefan.

"Me first!" shrieked Daniel, as they both struggled to squeeze through the doorway at the same time.

Dracula took a step forward. "Now, Renfield!" he called.

With that, a short plump man appeared outside the door. He had a thick moustache and round metal rimmed glasses that enhanced the cheeky glint in his eyes.

"Yes, Master," he said, as he pulled a net from

behind his back and threw it over the two frantically struggling thieves.

"Aaaah!" screamed Stefan, "They've got us!"

"What… what are you going to do?" asked Daniel, looking like he might cry.

The Count moved over to the candle, still flickering its soft golden light around the cellar and with a mischievous grin, blew it out.

CHAPTER 2

"There we are Inspector, we have your men," Count Dracula stood in the office of Inspector Constantine, the two thieves still trapped in the net at his feet.

"We caught them trying to make a withdrawal from the bank after closing time!" chuckled Renfield, poking Stefan with his finger.

Inspector Constantine stood up from behind his desk and walked over to the still struggling bundle on the floor. The Inspector had a set of bushy side whiskers that joined up to a thick moustache that almost hid his mouth. But that's where the hair ended as the top of his head was completely bald.

"My word, Count - you've done it again," he said. "We've been after this pair for months. We nick named them the Mole Men as they always tunnel in to wherever they commit their crime!"

"Glad to be of help," said Dracula, as he bowed slightly. "However, we must now return to Castle Dracula as the dawn will soon be upon us."

Inspector Constantine turned to look out of the window, and indeed could see the first glimpses of the morning sunlight on the horizon.

"Of course, Count Dracula. Thank you for helping to make the streets of Transylvania safe again, and…" but as he turned back he realised both the Count and Renfield had already gone, leaving him alone with the two terrified criminals.

*****

It was always a busy time for Renfield during the day, as his master slept soundly in his wooden coffin deep down in the crypt of Castle Dracula.

First he would dust away all the cobwebs that seemed to endlessly appear overnight, and then dig up all the weeds from the flower beds that grew around the castle moat, while at the same time feeding the crocodiles that lurked beneath the surface of the dark water. The windows would also need cleaning (all 150 of them) and the washing would need hanging out (it was amazing how many capes the Count went through).

After a non-stop morning, he was about to take a bite of his well-earned lunch when there was a loud shout from outside the castle. He rushed to the kitchen window and could see the postman running across the wooden drawbridge, being chased by a crocodile.

Renfield couldn't help chuckling to himself as he approached the huge oak front door and slid back the large iron bolt. No sooner was the door open than the postman dived inside, sweat pouring from his brow.

"Oh, Mr. Renfield!" he whimpered. "Can't you keep them brutes locked up!?"

"Come now, Joseph," said Renfield, "you know you simply have to be firm with them."

The crocodile poked its head inside, staring at the postman. It opened its mouth and dropped a small yellow ball which rolled to Renfield's feet. "See - he only wants to play with you."

Renfield threw the ball out into the moat, and the crocodile wagged its tail then ran and dived back into the murky water.

Joseph breathed a sigh of relief.

"I swear, Mr. Renfield, one of these days that beast is going to be the end of me!"

"Oh, you don't have to worry about Old Scaley - he's harmless."

"Still, I think I'd be the one who'd be armless if he had his chance!"

After a sit down and a drink to calm his nerves, Joseph handed over the mail and made his way quickly back across the drawbridge. Renfield sat down to read through the letters and discovered that one was from a family who were asking for the Count's help to solve a robbery. It explained how two nights ago, jewellery and a large teddy bear had been stolen from their home and as Renfield thought this was an unusual crime, he kept the letter to one side to show his Master later.

Soon the sun had worked its way across the sky and was starting to set behind the Transylvanian mountains. Down in the dark crypt, a coffin lid creaked open. Count Dracula slowly sat up, opened his eyes and looked round his gloomy surroundings.

"Renfield!" he called "Where are my slippers?"

A short time later, Dracula (now in his slippers) was sat in his favourite armchair in the study, drinking from a large glass of dark red liquid.

"You know, Renfield? I think maybe I should cut down on the pig's blood. My capes are starting to feel a little tight."

"Yes, Master," said Renfield, putting another log onto the roaring fireplace. "I'll make sure it's semi– skimmed next time."

Suddenly a loud knock echoed through the castle.

"A-ha! It would appear we have guests," said the Count, raising an eyebrow.

After their new visitors, a worried looking lady and a young girl, had made themselves comfortable on the sofa opposite Dracula, they began to tell him their problem.

"Last night we were robbed," said the lady, putting her arm around the young girl's shoulders, "and all of my jewellery was taken, as well as a teddy bear belonging to my daughter."

As soon as Renfield heard this he grabbed the letter that he'd opened earlier that day.

"This was last night?" he asked.

"Yes, Mr. Renfield," she replied. "The police have been at our house all day but have found no clues."

"This is very strange," continued Renfield, handing the letter to the Count. "This letter arrived today, which mentions a similar robbery that occurred two nights ago."

"Interesting," said Dracula, quickly reading the letter. "Please go on, Mrs...?"

"I am Mrs. Victoria Rosenbloom and this is my daughter Annalise. Last night someone invaded our house and took all the jewellery from my jewellery box. They didn't take anything else except for a new teddy bear belonging to Annalise."

The Count stood up and stepped over to the fireplace. "Was the teddy bear valuable?" he asked.

"No," said Mrs. Rosenbloom. "In fact my daughter had only had it for a day. Isn't that right, Annalise?"

The little girl looked up at the Count and nodded.

"I won it at the fair," she said softly. "I loved it because it was so fluffy and cuddly."

"It was nearly as big as Annalise herself, and quite heavy – my husband had to carry it home," said her mother. "In fact we were surprised they would give away such a big prize, as other people seemed to be winning small teddy bears."

"I see... and you say the police found nothing?" asked Dracula, becoming more intrigued.

"Yes, but one thing seemed to puzzle them. They discovered that the front door had been unlocked from the inside and left open. No other windows or doors had been tampered with, so it was as if the robber simply appeared in our house, stole our things and then walked out through the front door."

"Very well!" said Dracula. "I will investigate! Renfield, get the coach ready and take these delightful ladies home."

"Yes, Master."

"What is your address, Mrs. Rosenbloom? I will meet you there shortly."

"123 Castle View Gardens," she replied, standing up. "Oh thank you, your Lordship."

"Thank you, Count Dracula." said Annalise.

"It is a pleasure, my dear," said Dracula smiling. "And don't worry, we will get your things back!"

CHAPTER 3

Dracula stood at the top of the highest tower of the castle and looked out over the town of Transylvania, nestled at the foot of the dark and looming Carpathian Mountains. The small pin pricks of light from the town's gas lamps were like a reflection of the bright stars above. He loved the night time and how everything shimmered by the silvery light cast from the face of the moon.

Suddenly, he jumped off the battlements and plummeted downwards. As he rushed towards the ground he slowly raised his arms creating a kind of parachute with his cape, and then *POOF!* - he turned into a small bat and began to fly in the direction of the lights.

There was a lot of activity in the main square due to a travelling fair that was visiting the town. Each night, families would have fun on the rides and play games on the stalls for prizes. Dracula swooped down low to get a better look.

There was a strong smell of sweet food and hot chocolate - smells that would no doubt excite the town folk but were wasted on the Count. He could hear the laughs and screams of those riding on the carousel and the calls of stall owners trying to entice people to play their games.

With a smile on his bat lips and a flap of his wings he soared back up into the night sky and landed moments later in the garden of the Rosenbloom house. As he stepped out from the shadow of a large oak tree, he used his vampire powers to take on the shape of a large wolf.

He crept slowly around the exterior – inspecting the ground, studying each door and window carefully and sniffing for clues to how the crime was committed.

Soon afterwards he was seated next to Renfield in Mrs. Rosenbloom's living room (in his normal human form of course).

"Well, Mrs. Rosenbloom," he began. "I can see why the police were puzzled. There would appear to be no tracks at all approaching the house and no signs of anyone breaking in. The only footprints, other than those left by you and the police, begin at the front door and head off towards the town."

"But then how did they get in?" asked Mrs. Rosenbloom anxiously.

Dracula stood and began pacing across the room, his cape flowing behind him.

"At first I thought they may have come down the chimney," he continued, "but you have metal grills fixed over the top to prevent birds getting stuck, and I doubt our burglar is smaller than a bird. Plus it would have been impossible not to leave sooty footprints around the house."

"I checked the cellar, Master," said Renfield, "and there's no way anyone could have entered from there either."

"Mmmm… therefore we can deduce that the thief was already in the house."

"Are you saying that one of our servants committed the crime?" asked Mrs. Rosenbloom, shocked at the idea.

"No. The footprints from your servants all enter and leave through the back door and none of their prints match those at the front." Dracula moved to the large bay window and peered out into the darkness. "Judging from the size of the unknown footprints and the length of the stride, we are looking for a small thief, possibly even a child. That could possibly even explain the theft of the teddy bear."

"Why, that's amazing, your Lordship," said Mrs. Rosenbloom.

"That is not all," he continued. "Our intruder also left a particular scent which leads me to believe I know where he came from."

"Pray tell, where?"

Dracula turned back to face them and grinned. "The fair in the centre of town," he said, raising an eyebrow. "It was the smell of toffee apples."

CHAPTER 4

The fair was in full swing as Count Dracula and Renfield entered the market square.

"Renfield, it may be best if we split up. You go that way and I'll work my way round this way. We will meet up at the Ferris wheel."

"Yes, Master," replied Renfield, looking at the slow moving mass of people in his path. He turned back to the Count but he had vanished.

"I wish he wouldn't do that," said Renfield to himself and be began pushing his way through the crowd, looking for anyone acting suspiciously.

He noticed a smell that made him stop and sniff the air - toffee apples! If the Count was right, the toffee apple stall was the best place to start.

He pushed his way through the crowd until he reached the stall, and decided to buy one so he would look less suspicious as he inspected the area.

To one side was a brightly coloured tent where

you could have your photograph taken inside. Photography was still fairly new and only rich people could afford to buy a camera, so a long line of people queued outside as the chance to have a portrait taken didn't come about very often.

To the other side was a game stall with a sign that read:

'SHOOT THE INDIANS AND WIN A PRIZE!'

The back of this stall was painted to look like the American Wild West, and in front of this were small Red Indians figures going round on a slowly revolving track. In front of the stall was a small boy with a bow and arrow. He pulled back the bow string with all his might and let go - the arrow flew through the air and thudded into the wooden background without hitting any of the Indians.

"Oh... Nice try my young lad, but no prize for you," said the stall owner - a giant of a man with a huge barrel chest and arms as thick as tree trunks. He had a shaved head and wore braces to hold up his trousers.

"Better luck next time!" he said, as he took back the bow and then called out to the crowd. "Roll up! Roll up! Try your hand at shooting some pesky Injuns!"

An old crooked man approached the stall with a young pretty girl. They were both very thin and looked quite poor.

"Grand Papa?" the girl asked. "Could I please have a go at this game?"

"Of course you can, my angel," said the old man, putting his hand into his pocket. He pulled out a coin and handed it to the stall owner. "But that's my last penny. We'll have to go home after this."

The girl gave a little skip then picked up the bow

and arrow and took careful aim. She let the arrow fly and it knocked over one of the slowly moving figures.

"I hit it!" she squealed.

"You certainly did, little lady," said the stall owner as he handed her a small teddy bear. "Well done!"

The little girl giggled with delight and clutched her prize tightly as she walked away with her proud grandfather.

So this was where the teddy bears were coming from, thought Renfield. He pushed the still wrapped toffee apple into his pocket and crept round to the back of the stall to investigate. Quickly looking round to see that no-one was watching, he pulled back a large sheet and slid inside. He was now behind the Wild West stand where he could hear the stall owner on the other side calling out to the crowd. Scattered on the floor around him were boxes of small stuffed teddy bears. Nothing seemed out of the ordinary, until he noticed that draped over one of the boxes was what seemed to be a large teddy bear suit. He held it up and saw it had a zip running along its back, and was empty inside – there was no stuffing.

He had to let the Count know what he had discovered! Suddenly, there was a noise behind him and before he had chance to turn, something hit him over the head! Everything went black.

CHAPTER 5

Count Dracula wasn't having much luck. He had searched every stall he came across without uncovering any clues and was now stood waiting for Renfield at the foot of the Ferris.

He then noticed something peculiar – a few of the children passing him were carrying small teddy bears which they had won at the fair, yet none of them had a large bear like the one that the Rosenbloom family had won.

Dracula flapped his cape and turned into a bat, then flew up and perched on top of the Ferris wheel. Here he would have a better view to search for large teddies and his lost companion.

The seat that was now approaching the top of the wheel held a rather plump gentleman with very red cheeks, who was laughing and throwing nuts at the crowd below. He then caught sight of Dracula and stopped.

"Blow me!" he huffed. "A bloomin' bat! Get 'orf

this ride!" He grabbed a hand full of nuts and threw them at the Count, who took flight and dodged them easily.

"I wish you wouldn't do that," he said calmly, his red eyes burning bright.

"Upon my soul! It talks!" cried the rude man.

Dracula landed on the seat next to him and quick as a flash turned into a wolf. The man now screamed and tried to clamber away.

"I also bite!" snarled the Count.

The man then froze and looked down at his trousers, where a large wet patch had appeared between his legs.

"Oh dear," smiled Dracula, with a huge grin across his wolf face. "Looks like you've had a little accident." And with a *POOF!* - the Count turned back into a bat and circled over the crowd that were now laughing at the man with red cheeks and wet trousers.

Dracula chuckled to himself and then caught the smell of toffee apples in the air.

A-ha!, he thought, and followed the scent.

*****

Renfield was slowly coming to after being knocked unconscious. His hands and feet were tied and one of the small teddy bears had been stuffed into his mouth preventing him from speaking. His head ached but he could hear two people talking behind him.

A small whiny voice like that of a youth said, "I caught him snooping around!"

Renfield then recognized the second voice as the big man who ran the bow and arrow stall.

"Well..." said the stall owner, "I think a snooper

like this needs punishing, don't you?"

"Yeah!" chuckled the smaller voice.

"Then I'd best go see if we can get some customers to help with that!"

Renfield heard the stall owner lift the sheet and head outside. He shook his head to clear away the fuzziness and found that he was pressed up against a large wooden board covered in small holes, one of which was near his left eye. He squinted through and could make out the stall owner addressing the crowd, until an object moved in front of the hole and blocked his view for a second. This was followed by another, and another, and...

Renfield's heart sank as he realized where he was – strapped against the Wild West background with the Red Indian figures moving on their track in front of him!

Whoever played the game next would be firing arrows directly at him!

CHAPTER 6

Dracula hovered above the toffee apple stall but could see no sign of Renfield or anyone acting suspiciously.

A very well-dressed and obviously wealthy family approached one of the stalls below. The young boy looked up to his father hopefully.

"Can I have a go, Father?" he asked.

"Why not?" he replied, as he reached into his waistcoat pocket and pulled out a heavy looking purse. He produced a shiny coin and handed it over to the stall owner who Dracula could see was practically drooling over the size of the purse.

"Just shoot one of the Injuns to win a prize," he said, handing over the bow and arrow with an evil glint in his eye.

Renfield could only stare in terror as he saw the boy aim the arrow at the moving Indians, and of course straight at him. With a *WHOOSH!* the arrow was released and with a *THUD!* it pierced the wooden board - its pointed end narrowly missing Renfield's shoulder. He breathed a great sigh of relief.

The stall owner gave the boy another arrow.

"Here you go, my lad. Try another shot why don't you?" he said, smiling wickedly. The boy took aim once again and Renfield felt certain that this arrow would find its mark. *WHOOSH!* - the arrow shot forward just as Renfield's view was again blocked by one of the revolving Indians and this time he heard a loud *THUNK!*

"Oh, you missed!" cried the stall owner. "I mean, you hit.. you hit one of the Injuns! You win a prize!"

Dracula watched on as the big man stepped behind the large sheet at the back of the stall, and reappeared a moment later carrying a large stuffed teddy bear.

"So - We have a winner." said Dracula to himself, "A large teddy bear for a well to do family. Now I understand!"

He swooped down behind the stall and turned back into the Count. He could hear movement from behind the sheet and lifting the corner, peered inside. His eyes widened in horror at what he saw, and in a flash he had freed Renfield and removed the teddy bear from his mouth.

"Oh thank you, Master! I thought I was done for!"

"Quick, Renfield, we haven't a moment to lose."

Suddenly, the stall owner appeared from behind the sheet.

"What's going on 'ere!?" he growled.

"I'll take care of this fellow," bellowed the Count. "Renfield, you must catch that family and retrieve the large teddy bear before we lose them in the crowd!"

Without hesitation, Renfield darted off into the market square leaving Dracula to face the angry stall owner.

"I know who you are!" he said, eyeing the Count warily. "You're Count Dracula. I've heard about you and how you like to help the police."

He then grabbed a broken piece of wood from one of the boxes and held the sharp splintered end towards Dracula.

"Well... who's going to help you!?" he growled, and barreled forward stabbing his makeshift weapon at the Count.

Dracula span round at lightning speed with his foot raised, tripping his attacker and sending him sprawling out through the sheet. Dracula sprinted after him but barely had enough time to shift his body back as the sharpened wooden stake sliced through the air in front of him.

"I've thought up a new game," roared his assailant. "Stake a vampire and win a prize!"

With that, he thrust his stake again towards Dracula's chest. The Count nimbly swerved the advance but the weapon caught his cape and ripped a hole in the material, spinning him off balance against the side of the tent where people were queuing to have their photograph taken.

The stall owner pounced forward, relentlessly swinging his makeshift weapon and the Count could only drop to the ground to dodge the onslaught. For a big man, he could certainly move fast and with nowhere else to go Count Dracula rolled under the side of the tent just as the wooden stake stabbed into the ground where he had been.

Dracula was now looking up at a shocked husband and wife who moments before had been happily posing for a photograph. Bending over behind the large bellows camera, was the photographer with his head under a large black cloth.

"And hold that pose, please," he said, raising a flash plate above his head. With a roar the huge brute tore a hole through the side of the tent and jumped inside, sending the husband and wife screaming to the safety of the crowd outside.

"And smile," said the photographer, still with his head covered, completely unaware of the events taking place before him.

Dracula scrambled away from his foe until he was at the photographer's feet. It was all happening too fast; the Count didn't even have enough concentration time to transform into a wolf or bat to help him escape the lumbering stall owner.

"Time to claim my prize!" he snarled as he raised his stake for one last thrust directly at the Count's heart.

CHAPTER 7

Just as the sharp point of the wooden stake was arcing towards the Count's chest, there was a loud *PUFF!* and for a brief moment the tent was awash with intense bright light. The photographer had taken his photo and the flash plate had erupted, blinding the monster of a man who was stood directly in front of the camera and who now staggered backwards covering his face with his hands.

"My eyes!" he screamed. "I can't see!"

This was just the chance the Count needed. He summoned up his powers and turned into a wolf, then pounced upon the villain. His powerful jaw knocked the wooden stake to the floor and he stood on all fours over his enemy, who was now cowering on his back in terror.

"Mercy!" he pleaded, as he felt the Count's hot breath, and saw his sharp canine teeth inches away from his face.

"Lovely - !" said the photographer as he brought his head out from under the cloth. His bottom jaw dropped as for the first time he realised that the married couple he had expected to see had now been replaced by a huge wolf with blazing red eyes, looking like it was about to tuck into a huge man shaped dinner!

"I say!" he exclaimed.

Renfield had been frantically searching for the family who had just won the large teddy bear. He couldn't understand why it was so important but he knew that the Count would have his reasons.

Just when he thought he would have to give up, he spotted them near the exit. He could see the father struggling to carry the large bear over his shoulder.

"Stop!" called Renfield, as he reached them. "I can't allow you to take that bear."

"What is the meaning of this?" demanded the father.

"I must insist," said Renfield as he grabbed one of the bear's legs.

"Take your hands off my bear, you bounder!" cried the man, clutching the bear's head.

The surrounding crowd stared on in shock at the

two men pulling at either end of the bear. They were shocked even further when the bear gave a loud yelp of pain – "Owww!"

Surprised, both men let go and the teddy fell heavily to the floor, at which point it jumped to its feet and ran off through the crowd.

"Stop that teddy bear!" cried Renfield, heading off in hot pursuit. He struggled to keep up as it was smaller than him and could slip through the mass of people with greater ease, but he soon caught up and managed to grab hold of one of its furry ears.

"Get off me!" squeaked a small voice from inside the bear. It swung one of its paws at Renfield's head, who just had time to duck but lost his grip on the bear's ear. The teddy ran to the nearest stall and picked up a hammer that people had been using to test their strength by striking a lever that would ring a large bell. The bear swung the hammer at Renfield who managed to dodge out of the way.

"Drop that hammer, you naughty bear!" ordered Renfield, keeping just far enough away to avoid being hit.

"Never!" squeaked the bear charging forward with the hammer held high over its head. Renfield retreated backwards until he came up against the post which held the bell at the top. He realised he had nowhere left to go!

Then he remembered – the toffee apple in his pocket! He pulled off the wrapper and threw the sticky sweet at the oncoming bear. It stuck fast to on one of its furry legs and as the bear took another step, became glued against the other leg. Renfield calmly stepped out of the way as the bear lost its balance, dropped the hammer and crashed against the lever which hit the bell with a loud *CLANG!*

*****

Dracula and Renfield were stood with Inspector Constantine and two police constables in the town square, now quiet after the fair had been closed. Sat in front of them looking thoroughly miserable were the stall owner and teddy bear, in iron handcuffs.

"I have to confess," said Constantine, "I'm still not sure what's been going on. Why do we have a bear in custody?"

"It's simple, Inspector," said Dracula, pulling at the long tear that ran down his cape, "these two are responsible for the robberies over the last few nights and no doubt for many more in other towns that this travelling fair has visited."

"Well, I can believe that of this big ruffian, but what on earth has his teddy bear got to do with it?"

"This is no teddy bear, Inspector," said Dracula as he pulled the zip down the bear's back. The costume fell away to reveal a very short angry man, who glared at them with rage.

"Why, that's Shorty Wilson!" exclaimed Constantine. "He's wanted all over Eastern Europe."

"Quite," continued the Count. "Each night this pair would run their stall, waiting for their perfect victim. Should anyone poor win their game they would be given a small bear, but a child from a wealthy family would win the jackpot - Mr Wilson here dressed up in the large teddy bear costume.

Once inside the family's home, he would wait for the household to retire to bed before stealing their jewels and simply walking out the front door."

"Fantastic!" beamed Inspector Constantine. "You've done it again, my dear Count. And not forgetting your part in all this, Mr. Renfield."

"Yes - I would be lost without my trusty Renfield by my side," smiled the Count. "But I'm afraid we are once again cut short by the approaching dawn. Come, Renfield - we must return to Castle Dracula. I have a cape that needs mending!"

"Yes, Master," replied the happy Renfield.

As they headed back to their waiting coach and horses, Dracula reached into his pocket.

"Oh, I almost forgot, my friend. Here is a souvenir of our adventure for you."

"What is it?"

The Count pulled out a black and white photograph and handed it to Renfield.

"My new friend the photographer let me have it. It's the photograph he took of our large ugly acquaintance during our scuffle earlier."

Renfield looked at the image in his hand - the photo showed the brutes face just as the flash had gone off.

The Count was right, it was very large and very ugly.

"Not one for the family album, Master," smiled Renfield.

Dracula Investigates...
The Invisible Flan

It was a long time ago when our story began
When Professor Xavier made an invisible flan.
The idea for which seems a terrible waste
A dessert you can't see but are able to taste.

The formula used he kept just to himself
In the hope that someday he could sell it for wealth.
But one afternoon, when he came home from fishing
He entered his lab, but the flan had gone missing.

Who could have done such a terrible crime?
And who would be able to find out in time?
For if somebody else now the flan they did hold
They could sell it themselves for a fortune in gold.

Professor Xavier knew just who to call
Count Dracula, the greatest detective of all.
As soon as the sun had gone down in the west
The Count did appear to do what he did best.

He searched round the lab in the hope of a clue
Something to help him, a footprint or two?
But nothing he saw seemed to be out of place
It was looking to be a mysterious case.

After all who could know of the incredible flan?
To scheme and think up such a dastardly plan.
No window was broken, all doors had good locks
Yet somehow the flan was removed from its box.

"It's no use!" cried Xavier "My flan can't be found!"
"Not so." said the Count still searching around.
"I'll turn into a wolf with a keen sense of smell
The flan isn't far from what I can tell."

Now down on all fours with his nose in the air
Dracula the wolf knew the flan was still there.
"The mystery is solved!" he called out with a smile
"The flan is not lost; it's been here all the while.

"Well I'm lost." said the Prof. "No mistake about that."
And then he sat down with a very loud *SPLAT!*
"Come, come." said the Count, "No need to look glum.
I think you will find it's all over your bum!"

Dracula Investigates...
The Mystery of the Sax Museum

"Oh, thank goodness you've arrived, Count Dracula!" said the curator of the Sax Museum, wiping his already sweating brow with a handkerchief. He pulled open the large front door to allow both Dracula and Renfield to enter the huge marble hallway, as they shook the rain from their clothes.

"A horrible night out there," smiled the Count.

"Yes indeed sir, I'm so grateful you could venture out to help me," replied the curator. He was a short, plump man, well dressed in a purple velvet suit, his chin almost hidden by an extremely frilly shirt.

"What seems to be the problem, Mr...?" asked Renfield, taking in the extravagant surroundings.

"I am Mr. Kovac and I run this museum. We have the largest collection of saxophones in all Eastern Europe. However, earlier this evening I discovered that our most prized possession had been stolen! It was a unique piece created by the great Adolphe Sax himself in 1846 – a solid gold, diamond studded saxophone. It is quite priceless!"

The little man appeared ready to faint and had to lean against one of the large marble pillars that seemed to reach up to the heavens above.

"Well now, Mr. Kovac - what can you tell us about the events leading up to the crime?" asked the Count gently. Kovac took several deep breaths to calm himself and then began to describe what had occurred that evening.

"The museum was open as usual for the day," he began, pulling at his collar, "and when closing time came at six o'clock everything was in its place. The night time security guards arrived and I went to my office to finish up some paper work. An hour later, at about seven o'clock, I went for a wander to stretch my legs. I saw that the saxophone was in its place up on the wall in the main gallery at that time. I checked in with the guards doing their rounds and then went back to my office."

Again, the emotion began to swell in the little man's voice and he had to fight back tears.

"As you may know," he continued, "it started to rain heavily at about eight o'clock, so I rushed outside to bring in the board which displays our opening times. That was the only time the front door was open and I am the only one with a key. I remember passing one of the guards in the hall as I went back to my office. I had been there for no more than half an hour when another one of our guards burst in shouting that the golden saxophone had gone missing!"

"So that would be about 8:30?" asked Renfield.

"That is correct. I immediately ran to the main gallery and to my horror saw that it had indeed been stolen."

"Could we take a look at the scene of the crime?" asked the Count.

Moments later they were stood in the large main gallery, its wood panelled walls lined with many different varieties of saxophone, some in glass display cases and some on wooden stands. suspended high above their heads was an empty glass cabinet, where the priceless saxophone had been displayed.

"The saxophone was certainly kept well out of reach," observed Dracula studying the room.

"Indeed yes," said Kovac. "We couldn't allow members of the public to touch it."

Dracula heard the sound of heavy rainfall coming through a partially open window at the far end of the gallery. "Is that window normally left open?" he asked.

"Heavens, no. I only noticed it was open after the crime had been discovered but left it just as it was. It can only be opened from the inside and in fact only opens a small amount as you can see - certainly not enough for anyone to fit through."

"Yes, you are right there," said Renfield writing in his notebook. "But it's big enough to fit a saxophone through."

"The guards," said Dracula pacing around the room. "Tell me about them - would they have any reason to commit such a crime against their employer?"

"I believe they do indeed! We have three night time security guards, Varga (who discovered the crime), Molnar and Rozman. They have worked at the museum for years but were all recently disciplined for breaking the rules. Varga was caught eating sandwiches in the store room at the back of the museum last week, Molnar was late for work on Wednesday and Rozman was caught sleeping on the job last night. They were all given a good telling off and I took a week's wages off them all as punishment. Since there is no way for anyone to have entered the museum, I'm sure one of them has committed the crime, but which one?"

"Could I meet with them?" asked Dracula.

"Of course," Kovac pulled on a bell rope which

hung down in the corner of the room and soon afterwards all three guards were lined up in the gallery in front of the Count and Renfield.

Varga was a very short fat man whose belly almost burst out of his uniform on which Dracula spotted crumbs visible on the collar. Next to him stood Rozman, an extremely tall and thin man with trousers that barely reached his ankles. Dracula observed that one of his sleeves was slightly wet. The last guard, Molnar was a slim man of average height and wore a watch on a chain round his neck which Dracula noticed was running an hour slow.

"Mr. Varga. I understand that you discovered the theft?" asked the Count, slowly walking up and down in front of the guards.

"Yes sir. I was doing my rounds of the ground floor and when I entered the main gallery I looked up and saw that the gold saxophone was missing from its display case. I immediately ran to the office to tell Mr. Kovac."

"Can you also explain why you have what appear to be the remains of a bacon sandwich on your uniform?"

"Erm… I must have made a bit of a mess when I ate my dinner before coming to work."

Dracula turned to face the second guard. "Mr. Rozman. Can you tell us your whereabouts during the evening?"

"I was upstairs patrolling the upper gallery. I heard a noise from downstairs as if someone had forced open a window but by the time I ran down here the crime had already been discovered."

"And may I ask why your sleeve appears to be damp?"

"I got caught in the rain on the way to work this evening."

Dracula turned to face the final guard. "And finally, Mr. Molnar, where were you while the crime was being committed?"

"I was in the main hall. I saw Mr Kovac bring the sign in from outside at about 7 o'clock when the rain started."

"Very well!" exclaimed Dracula as he turned to the museum owner with a glint in his eye. "I now know who did it and where the saxophone is."

Do you know which of the guards stole the golden saxophone and where it is now?

Was it Varga, Rozman or Molnar?

Turn to the next page to find out!!

"The thief is none other than Rozman," said Count Dracula pointing at the stunned security guard.

"How did you know, Master?" asked Renfield.

"Elementary, my dear Renfield," smiled the Count. "Whoever stole the golden saxophone had to be tall enough to reach it, since it was kept in the cabinet high up on the gallery wall. Mr. Varga here is far too short which leaves Molnar and Rozman, and even Molnar may have struggled being only of medium height. Rozman claims to have been caught in the rain on the way to work and that this is why the sleeve of his uniform is wet, and yet we know it didn't start raining until 8 o'clock when the guards were already in the building - the time when Mr. Kovac brought in the museum sign. Molnar saw him in the main hall at what he thought was 7 o'clock. It was in fact 8 o'clock as Molnar's watch is an hour slow; this no doubt being as to why he was late for work earlier in the week."

Molnar looked at his watch, scratching his head.

"Rozman was upstairs," continued Dracula, "but would have had plenty of time to creep down to the main gallery and steal the saxophone while Varga was in the store room once again snacking on a sandwich, the crumbs of which are visible on his uniform."

Varga looked over at Kovak, his cheeks bright red with guilt.

"But where is the saxophone?" whimpered Mr. Kovak, "Rozman couldn't have left the museum as I have the only key to the door."

"Rozman opened the small window at the end of the gallery and dropped the saxophone into the bushes outside. It was raining heavily at that time and this is when his sleeve became wet. He planned to simply pick it up on his way home in the early morning before any visitors arrived."

"Oh... thank you, Count Dracula!" exclaimed Kovak pushing his handkerchief back into his top pocket, "Varga, detain Rozman and watch him while Molnar here runs into town to notify the police."

A short time later Inspector Constantine had arrived to take the prisoner away and Kovak had retrieved the saxophone from its hiding place outside the gallery window.

Back at Castle Dracula the Count was once again sat in his favourite arm chair in front of a roaring fire enjoying a nice glass of semi–skimmed pig's blood.

So... how did you do? Did you solve the crime just like the Count?

Dracula Investigates...
The Ghost of Prankenstein

Prankenstein was known for his terrible jokes,
tricks and stunts played on many town folks.
But the worst one of all if I had to decide,
was the time that the poor fellow actually died.

He'd once scared his neighbours by playing the fool,
dressed as a werewolf which was terribly cruel.
And Old Farmer Topol had fallen quite faint,
when he'd found all his cattle had been covered in paint.

The trickster had often made claims as a liar,
and once had pretended the town was on fire.
People had rushed from their houses to flee,
to find him stood laughing and grinning with glee.

Many had tried to change his bad ways,
only to have him pull pranks within days.
But the final straw came when he said he could fly,
and had climbed to the top of the town hall to try.

"I'll turn into a bat like the great Count can do!"
he had called from above and in everyone's view.
So out into the night he had jumped as they feared,
and in front of their eyes he had just disappeared.

Could it be true, could he really have changed,
into a bat as the mad fool had claimed?
In the river below he must surely have drowned,
but after a search no body was found.

Count Dracula and I were then called to the case,
after Prankenstein's fall from such a high place.
"It's a stunt!" said the townsfolk, "He's surely alive!
and has fooled us somehow with that terrible dive."

But the Count found no clue of where he could be,
and felt that he must have been washed out to sea.
The following days everyone was on edge,
casting an eye at the now famous ledge.

Would he simply return to continue his fun,
to play out his jokes and annoy everyone?
But the people forgot as the months passed on by,
and the legend of Prankenstein started to die.

Until one dark night he was seen for a while,
wandering alone, a phantom, no smile.
Now every year on the date of his fall,
his ghost is seen walking along the town wall.

It would seem that the joke is truly on him,
no more will he laugh with that terrible grin.
But the people took pity upon the sad spirit,
and throw him a party each year on his visit.

Dracula Investigates...

The Puzzle Pages

The Count needs your help to solve these puzzles?

The Castle Maze!

The sun is almost up!

Can you help Dracula find his way through the maze

and back to his coffin before it's too late?

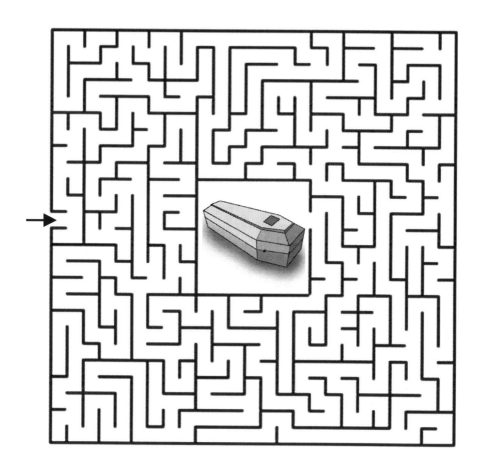

Wicked Word Search!

Search the puzzle and see if you can spot the words from

the bottom of the page

W	I	O	X	D	Z	W	G	N	A	M	U	I	W	G
X	I	N	T	G	O	K	T	F	S	O	M	O	O	V
P	W	R	S	R	C	K	C	B	L	O	O	D	L	J
F	A	Q	H	P	A	G	O	N	A	N	J	H	F	U
U	X	Y	B	H	E	N	N	Y	F	I	L	V	L	D
G	G	C	X	L	N	C	S	Q	R	N	O	E	A	R
R	R	O	K	L	R	A	T	Y	O	H	K	K	C	A
V	E	U	O	J	A	S	A	O	L	T	K	C	Q	C
L	P	N	Z	G	R	T	N	J	R	V	V	V	I	U
N	R	T	F	C	U	L	T	R	L	G	A	Y	Y	L
S	E	V	N	I	S	E	I	R	L	W	T	N	K	A
K	C	P	L	F	E	X	N	P	F	U	X	E	I	O
O	Y	H	O	A	V	L	E	S	Z	L	L	Q	X	A
J	J	N	E	P	E	M	D	W	L	X	E	K	J	U
Q	V	K	U	T	C	O	F	F	I	N	E	Y	A	Q

BLOOD	WOLF	MOON
DRACULA	CONSTANTINE	COFFIN
RENFIELD	BAT	COUNT
TRANSYLVANIA	INSPECTOR	CASTLE

Spot the Difference!

Can you find 10 things that are different

in the second picture below?

The
Puzzle
Solutions!

Turn the page to find the answers...

The Castle Maze!

Wicked Word Search

Spot the Difference!

ABOUT THE AUTHOR

Andy Bruce started out his creative journey at an early age through drawing and soon discovered a hidden talent for cartooning. Through school and college he used his illustrating skills to create both cartoons and short stories for school/college magazines.

More recently he has teamed up with lifelong friend Dave Blake (a talented author) who has published several children's short stories and poems and who Andy has helped to bring the iconic characters of "Duke Palooka", "Quentin DeVere", "Sebastian", "Poe" and "Atticus Wolf" to life.

As well as illustrating, Andy co wrote "The Dog Who Lost His Bark" with Dave before finally starting his first solo project "Dracula Investigates..."

To keep up to date with Dracula news, flap on over and like our Facebook page:

www.facebook.com/draculainvestigates

Or to find out about our other titles, visit:

www.kapasun.com/creations

Printed in Great Britain
by Amazon